The

Striders

Team

A
Play
by

ivey

The Striders Team

Copyright 2022
        by
Ivey McCray

First Edition
All rights reserved.

No part of this book is to be
reproduced or transmitted in any form or by
any means without written permission from
the author.

BELLE CHASE BOOKS
Printed in United States
Washington, D.C.

ISBN 979-8-218-02414-7

belle.chase@mail.com

Contents

TIME and PLACE

It is early evening, hours before the final race at a major indoor invitational track meet in Oakland, California.

SETTING

Downstate center/is a locker room with a long wooden bench and a set of four metal lockers behind it.

The track of four lanes runs around the circumference of the stage area, marked by multi colors with horizontal lines staggered across each to indicate start lines.

There are two entrances/exits. One is downstage left that leads to and from the locker area. The other is downstage right for the track entrances and exits.

SOUND

Music is heard throughout the play. Hip hop, R&B, Salsa, Orchestra, drums, flutes, violins, and variation of jazz. intermixed with sounds of crowds, speakers, slamming locker doors, whistles.

CHARACTERS

In Order of Appearance

COACH
Founder of the Striders ,a private track and field club. He is an older male who still has an athletic appearance. He wears casual business attire, blazer jacket, trouser, and sneakers.

PORSCHE (Breeze)
Star runner, anchor runner for relay

HOLLY (Oops)
Third runner in the relay

RASHIDA (Hot Rod)
Second runner in the relay

JAZMINE(Speed)
Top runner, and lead runner for relay

BUD
Trainer who is a younger energetic man who wears a sports track suit

LOUDSPEAKER
Microphoned voice offstage

ACT I

PROLOGUE

Lights rises on PORSCHE downstage right. She does stretch exercises.

Porsche

(*S o f t l y   c o u n t i n g ,   h e a v y breathing*)...three...four... six... What fairy tale lights dangling like pearls around the lake (*Stops and looks out*) Magical. One more race, Striders. Then I am free. (*Exercises again*) One, two, three, four. (*Stops again*) How can I win tonight? My last race with the team. Pray. Prayers to the ground---allow me to glide through space, raise me to the sky above. (*Shrugs shoulder to release tension*) Let my breath be soothing over my aching body as I move to the finish line. Let each step be lighter and lighter. Win be with me (*Her exercises are become rapid*) There is only me. I have to win me. (*She jogs the track and exits*)

The COACH enters the track opposite from where PORSCHE exits. The stage is dark except the spotlights that follow him slowly walking the track. Once in front of the locker area, he poses as if passing off a baton. A painful moan is heard off stage, causing him to pull up quickly, as if he pulled a muscle. He stamps his foot several times to shake off the perceived pain, then walks briskly back to the exit he entered.

BLACKOUT

Scene
1

Lights rise on the locker room. HOLLY, RASHIDA and JAZMINE enter wearing business casual clothes. They carry their tracksuits and sneakers in gym bags.

Holly

(*Excited*) Yes, yes, yes. We are the best. Yea! (*Takes things out of bag and lines on bench*)

Jazmine

(*Stops short, drops gym bag and surveys lockers*) Can't believe it! The lockers are still beat up and ugly as when I ran here in high school. ugh-- Grungy.

Rashida

What did you expect, a Hollywood dressing room. They look like all the lockers we've been in around the country.

Holly

And she says the same about each. What's with you, Speed? Are you claustrophobic?

Jazmine

This is different. Oakland is hometown. I was told there was going to get a real welcome. Said, there was a special surprise waiting for me.

Holly

Like what? (*Holds arms out to block RASHIDA who is about to sit on bench*) No, no, no. The bench is mine!

Jazmine

A banner with my name on that wall. (*Selects and opens locker and begins to undress*) Break the record. Can you see it. Right there. (*Spreading an imaginary banner with her hands*)

Rashida

OOPS! Can you stop spreading all your junk in some weird routine.

Holly

This precious stuff is not junk. (*Takes each item from bag, piece by piece and lays each on the bench in a calculated fashion*) I have to see if I packed everything I need.

Rashida

(*Moves to locker*) How did you forget anything, Holly? You took all afternoon to pack it at the hotel fifteen minutes ago.

Holly

So. (*Takes a sketch pad from bag*) Look Ra.

Speed. These are my designs for Strider's new outfits. Coach said he'll look at them tonight.

Jazmine

(*Looks at them briefly*) Not bad.

Holly

Once the Striders race in them, I will become rich. Teams will call me from all other the world to design for them.
Look Ra. Like the color? (*Holding the pad up to RASHIDA's face*)

Rashida

Geez, Oops, out of my face. FOCUS.

Jazmine

Dresses, what a pain! I hate getting dressed up to come into lockers like this to undress. All the other teams arrive suited.

Rashida

We're here to win, not whine. Concentrate on your race.

Jazmine

I know how to calculate my race, Rashida. I won two state championships without you or the team. (*Pulling off dress*) You could try to bring him up to modern times. So what if we are independents, don't need to look like church girls.

Rashida

Just stop talking to me. (*Completely suites, she lays a prayer cloth on the floor to sit on*)

Holly

Hey, Speed. My mom gave me the Express on the way in. There's a write up about you, the team coming back to California for the finals. There was something about the Coach, too.

Jazmine

I'm thinking of joining another running club. A few recruiters have called.

Holly
Any about college offers?
Jazmine
Waiting. Still in shape to run for the Olympics.
Holly
(*Pulls out a newspaper from bag*) Says, the Bay has scored with a major track meet of national importance. They are ready, new stadium, new roads, new lights.
Jazmine
All LIES.
Holly
What makes it spectacular is the Striders who run races with Olympic legs—yay–yay--yay!
Jazmine
Where's my name? (*Looks over her shoulder*)
Holly
Continues to read) -moved by the vision

of the self- made man, the independent. Coach Campbell. The former track man from Texas who held local clinics, slowly building a club of 20- 30 regular athletes each year, working with kids in juvenile and foster house--- abusing alcohol...da-da–da..has an underdog team competing against deep pocket colleges. Now with two superb runners and a too hot to touch relay, he is cashing in. Cashing in? What?

Jazmine

Mean's–let me see the paper---means he's pocketing money.

Holly

He is acting strange. I think he's afraid of that sportswriter, who keeps trying to talk to us.

Rashida

(*Begins to chant away from the others*) Omm.omm...om.

Holly

(*Takes back paper*) Wait, wait, I have to see my (*Reads paper*) My horoscope--today says, sudden change brings new beginnings.

Jazmine

What else would come after a change. I don't see my name. (*Tosses paper back. Returns to suiting up*)

Rashida

(*Softly chants*) om..om...om..tat...sat...

Holly

Listen—you're a Gemini. It says. Make a wish three times, then a dream will come true. So, say a wish.

Jazmine

I want to win. (*Under breath*) I want to beat her just once.

Rashida

(Loudly)ooommmmmmmmmmmMM.

Holly

(*Tosses paper, stands over items on bench*)
Socks...toothbrush, comb, my sneakers.
My—hummh. Something's out of order.
(*Re-packs gym bag, then takes out each item
and lays on the bench again*)

Jazmine

Because you put the track suit on your
body not the bench.

Holly

I have a special order to control changing
from myself to another.

Jazmine

(*Picks up a toothbrush*) Sounds like
superstition. If you need this, a
toothbrush. You're lost, Oops.
Absolutely a loss.

Holly

My smile must be clean and fresh for
photographers, my fans.

Rashida

ommmommmmmmoOMMMM.

(*Then silence*)

Jazmine

(*Notices RASHIDA*) What is Hot Rod doing?

Holly

You know, the Om thing she does before a race. (*Still looking over her suit arrangement on the bench*)

Jazmine

(*Kneeling next to her*) Hey Ra, Ra, what's happening? You okay? (*Tapping her shoulder*)

Rashida

(*Eyes closed, yells without moving*) CAN I CONCENTRATE!!!!!

Jazmine

(*Jumps back playfully*) Well, don't rise on your haunches and kick air about it. Only wanted to know why you were moaning.

Holly

AAAHHH, my glove! How can I run. I'm not running.

Rashida

Quiet!

Holly

Where's Porsche? She has the match. need it. Rashida, where is Porsche?

Jazmine

(*Sits on bench to put on sneakers*) She could be with the Coach...maybe with Buddd. Know you have a crush on him.

Rashida

Ooooommmmmmm.

Holly

So what. Rashida, where's Breeze?

Rashida

(*Annoyed, stops her prayer, rises*) You find her. (*Sits on the edge to put on her sneakers, pushing some of HOLLY's things onto the*

floor)
> **Holly**
Get up! You're sitting on my lineup.
> **Rashida**
You need to pray on it, Oops. Find some poetry in life, will you.
> **Holly**
Where's Porsche?
> **Rashida**
Haven't seen her all day. She left the room early.
> **Jazmine**
Heard some L.A. runners say they ran past her around the lake this morning.

> *PORSCHE enters wearing the team's sweats. She moves slowly to bench.*

> **Jazmine**
How do you rate----------

PORSCHE moves HOLLY's things to sit on bench.

Holly

Watch ! Don't sit on my things!

Jazmine

---coming in with sweats, <u>and</u> LATE. When we have to dress up.

Porsche

Always on time to beat you. Kiss off, Speed. Has Bud been in yet? (*Takes off sweat jacket*)

Rashida

Hey, legs up y'all. There's a third waiting to flash both of you out at the finish.

Jazmine

I'm alright. It's all in the bank. She has to hear my value, time to time. (*Puts foot on bench to rock it*)

Holly

Stop, Speed.

Porsche

(*Twist foot, as she takes off sweat pants. She moans*) Has Bud been in? awwhh–my foot.

Holly

Why do you want Bud?

Rashida

Why are you undressing? Are you hurt?

Porsche

Slides out of her sweat pants) It's hot in here.

The runners freeze.

LIGHTS OUT

Scene
2

Lights on COACH and BUD standing on the track right stage. COACH has a clip board and stop watch. BUD carries an athletic bag with towels and watches.

Coach

Feels good to be here tonight. Years of sweat to move into the big invitational meet. First time officials look me in the eyes when they speak. (*Looks over a sheet on a clip board*) Anyway, looking at yesterday's practice, I think the relay's times slipped. I have an idea to improve their speed. Let's get them out for a short work out.

Bud

Think we pushed them pretty hard this week.

Coach

Need peak performance tonight, Bud. (*Strolls downstage, looking over the audience*) Every official in track and field is watching, wondering how I got my club here. I want my team running better than they can.

Bud

(*Strolls alongside*) Tonight's an easy win.

Coach

No win is easy.

Bud

The team is strong–but tense. Porsche complains—

Coach

(*Cuts Bud off, indifferent and annoyed*) She wants to ride her winning streak. She gets anxious before major races.

Bud

Yesterday, I had to work out severe muscle spasms in her legs.

Coach

(*Inattentive*)---Her diet's off. Give her more calcium-magnesium. Keep her rubbed down and whatever else you must do as a trainer.

Bud

And the others? They are breaking. There's no reason to worry over losing.

Coach

It's win, Bud. Nothing else. Tonight's sold out to see my team, my runners, the Striders. I care about each runners...their bodies, the food they eat, how they sleep and with whom. Most of all how they race. I learn what they expect and I give, and give,and give. The only thanks I ask for-- is that they run their best to keep it coming.

Bud

Breeze is different.

Coach

Very different. (*Turns to face Bud*) Over and over in my head, I trained her before she joined my team. Even before I met her. I knew what my runner needs and doesn't. My only want is watching her pull the track under her feet. She's not peaking enough for me.

Bud

No problem, but there is talk you're dropping your Strider's team for a college position.

Coach

Wherever I go, I earned it. Give me a watch. (*Hands him a stopwatch*)

Bud

Gotcha. This practice is not necessary. A little kindness goes a long way.

Coach

I hear you, Bud. We'll make them stronger. My way, maybe your way. (*Walks away from BUD to the opposite side of track*) LET'S GO RUNNERS! ON THE TRACK!

Lights lower as the men freeze.

Scene 3

Lights rise again in the locker. Everyone moves about quickly, throwing their last things into lockers.

Holly

Wait up, Speed.

Jazmine

(*Slams locker shut*) Can't wait (*Exits*)

Porsche

What's happening? We never practice before a race?

Rashida

Probably a warm-up.

Porsche

Can't do it.

Holly

Yeah, you can.

Bud

(*Calls again*) Let's go runners!

Holly

Do it Breeze. It's nothing. (*Raises hand for high five*) Give me a bump. (*Raises fist for PORSCHE to bump. Then exits*)

Porsche

This is robot running.

Rashida

(*Putting on sneakers*) Why are you boo-hooing. You run before meets anyway.

Porsche

Tonight's different. It's a burn out.

Rashida

Can't burn. If we don't win tonight, it's over for another year before we get in these games. (*Throwing everything into her*

---

locker.) The Coach's been on fire since we returned to California.

Porsche

I don't think we will win.

Rashida

We will. We have to. (*Exits*)

> *HOLLY enters the track but stands next to BUD. JAZMINE is on the track stretching her legs.*

Coach

(*At entrance waiting for the other runners*) Feet on the track, Holly!

Holly

Waiting for Breeze and Ra.

Coach

Runners never wait. Go!

> *RASHIDA enters the track.*

Coach

Where's Porsche?

Rashida

(*Shrugs*) Give her a minute.

> *Steps on track joining HOLLY and JAZMINE who are at the staggered track lines ready to run.*

Porsche

(*Puts sweat hood back on*) Can't race, now. Coach has to accept it. It's over. (*She rises, testing her foot*) Why should I let them see me fall, laugh and clap at my stumble. How can I pretend? The body can't lie. (*She slowly exits*)

> *Lights off as the lockers are removed from the stage. Lights rise on the track. Music rises as individual spotlights showcase each runner as they mime running. They*

move from spotlight to spotlight. Each light fades as they move pass it. The lights create synchronized wavelike movement as the runners move with elbows and hand stroking space and knees rising and feet forward. It is breathless in appearance. Yet the sounds of their breaths accentuate the beat of the music. PORSCHE enters the track with hood over her head just before JAZMINE passes.

Jazmine
(*Nearing PORSCHE*) Out my way!
Porsche
Body be strong. Let winning rise in me.

COACH and BUD evenly pace their dialogue.

Coach
Run from your mind.

Bud

Keep it steady...move it slow. Only a warm-up.

Coach

RASHIDA, RELAX ...keep the hands loose!

Bud

You ain't dead yet, OOPS! Knees up!

HOLLY slows to the rear of the group, nearly stopping. After his call, she picks up some momentum but it's a struggle.

Porsche

Feeling my body riding the ground beneath me.

Coach

Bud, tape Holly's right knee!

Bud

Moving pretty, real nice...where's your focus. GET YOUR FOCUS, SPEED.

Porsche

Can't catch me. Can't catch me, pull the ground...override the edges of tiredness.

JAZMINE struggles to overtake PORSCHE.

Coach

Lovely. Bud, start your watch. PORSHE, GIVE ME MORE—SPEED.

Jazmine

I can beat her. I can.

Porsche

Strong. moving with force, loving the muscles sweating with speed---

Bud

Pure beauty, moving---

Coach

I GOT A CLOCK IN MY HAND! CAN YOU BEAT IT.

Porsche
Everything you do is to win.
Jazmine
Only mine! Take her-------
Coach
RUN! FASTER!
Bud
Hold up, Coach!
Porsche
WIN THE END-WIN IT.
Coach
FASTER!
Bud
Take the turn easy!

JAZMINE lunges to grab the back of PORSCHE's hood.

Coach AND Bud
STOP!

The two men click their watches, JAZMINE draws back, then takes a soft job around the track. COACH moves toward BUD. The other runners break from the mime-run to and go to the bench that now serves as bleachers. They freeze in the dark area.

Coach

What's your time?

Bud

(*Steps up to the approaching COACH*) Time? What about team spirit? Did you see Speed!?

Coach

Competition is good for a team.

He walks away to join RASHIDA and HOLLY sitting on bench. BUD follows glancing back at PORSCHE and JAZMINE who stops near PORSCHE.

Porsche

Don't ever touch me. Don't even act like it!
Ever!

Jazmine

Stay out of my way, clumsy. For TWO
YEARS, we've been running together. And
for TWO years I haven't won my race.

Porsche

Then change your run!

Jazmine

(*Breathy*) Hell no! The 200 is mine. I want to
win! I'm a better athlete than you.

Porsche

Too bad. Eat the fact--I am, FAST, because
your pain is getting treacherous.

Jazmine

Tired of finishing a second late in your
shadow.

Porsche

Feel you, Speed. You've pushed me to
shorter times and broken a few records

doing it—
Jazmine
But you take the tape!
Porsche
Because I run to beat me. Because there's no one in front of me, except me and my win. Keep trying to beat me and not yourself, you'll never win your race.
Coach
(*Calls*) Porsche! JAZMINE!
Jazmine
I will, and you're going to watch it happen.

Walks to sit with the others on bench.
PORSCHE rushes, then pulls up in pain
as she walks to the group.

Scene

4

Lights rise on the team as the two runners join the others. The sound of a marching band warming up for the opening ceremonies is heard with the muffled sounds of crowd noises.

PORSCHE slides on the bench next to the other runners. JAZMINE stands as does BUD to the side.

Holly
(*Quickly before anyone else*) Coach.

Bud

(*To PORSCHE*) Feeling ok, kid?

Coach

A few last pointers.

Holly

Coach, my designs------

Porsche

(*To BUD*) My ankle hurts ------

Coach

(*He stands before the group, holds his hand up to HOLLY*) One minute. Ra, let go. What are you holding onto?

Rashida

My concentration wanders. I drop my jaw to keep it loose. (*Demonstrates*) Aaahhh-----poofff. If only I could control my breathing like I want—

Jazmine

So help me, she should win from the noise alone.

Coach

Then you're trying too hard and it's straining your flow. Stop the arm flapping. Keep the shoulders down, straight lines. Anything outside of conciseness is against you. It's all about form. Stand. Show me good form.

Rashida

Coach, I know my form.

Coach

Then show me. Here, let me help you. (*Pulls her from the bleachers*)

Rashida

It's not going to make a difference here.

Coach

It won't if you doubt it. (*Places her in a running stance*) The knees come up high...leg out straight...then down. Keep the hips loose and easy. (*He places her arms and legs for her to maneuver them*)

Holly

(*Softly to self*) Bommp, bom take it to the

ground (*Slaps her hands together*)
Coach
The elbows are in a 90 degree angle. Faster they go, the faster the legs go. KEEP THE hands loose and easy. The breath will flow. Now move, show me.

RASHIDA does a quick jog in place.

Jazmine
(*Laughs*) Forget it.
Coach
Now make a mental picture of it. Got it?
Rashida
I think so. (*Sits on bleachers*)

HOLLY puts out a hand for a high five. RASHIDA waves it away.

Jazmine
Still shaky about my starts.

Bud
Your starts are fine, Speed. Just don't jump the gun.
Holly
And fall on your face like last year's double A trials. (*Smirks*) We lost time, watching you get up off your face.
Jazmine
Stepping on the wrong feet. Don't know how to start or stop.
Bud
Speed, you anticipate too much.
Jazmine
Not going to be last off the blocks.
Coach
Absolutely.
Bud
False starts are a loss of fuel.
Coach
You are good. Damn good. But timing has to be instinctive not imaginary.

Holly

Breeze and I have a great idea for passing.

Coach

Ah, another thing, gauge yourself in the 200.

Holly

Coach!?

Coach

Hold up Oops. It's mind over body. Save some for the finish stretch. Cause its deep sand, legs are heavy, with each stride you sink deeper, thinking you're ahead only to be swept under by others passing.

Holly

Porsche and I wear a pair of bright gloves.

Porsche

Oops hesitates on the hand off. It's a focus point for us.

Coach

Who forgot how to pass the baton?

Rashida

Really, Coach, we aren't air heads. We've won enough relays. Tonight is no different.

Coach

Every race is different. Unpredictable. I need to hear your hand off.

Rashida

Coach, we know—

Holly

Not robots, Coach–

Coach

The baton is no dope's game. Jazmine, show hands.

Jazmine

Come on—Not our first run.

Coach

Got it. Let's hear it.

As each runner calls out position they give a fist pound to the next runner.

Jazmine
First, right.
Rashida
Second, left.
Holly
THIRD, RIGHT (*Raises the left then the right, unsure*) Third, left---right (*Puts wrong hand up, then down, puts correct hand up*)
Porsche
Anchor, left. Other runners kick dirt in my face waiting for her.
Holly
Why should I run half your leg before you take it?
Porsche
I like to win. The lag wastes us. Rashida should be third.
Coach
I'll make that call.

Holly

What happens, is someone's hand doesn't take it fast enough.

Porsche

Put a little more out if you expect me to win.

Rashida

We all win the relay!

Jazmine

Nope, Oops and you try hard to win, but it's me and Porsch who break the relay records.

Rashida

If we didn't carry the baton between the two of you, you wouldn't win anything.

Coach

Hold up, the wins belong to all of us. There are times I feel they are mine and only mine. I run from Speed to Porsche. It belongs to no one.

This causes the team to twitch.

Coach

JUST DON'T DROP THAT BATON. If anyone does, we may as well walk home from the track right then.

Holly

Not all bad, C. A drop happened to Wilma Rudolph and she still won with a record in the '60 Olympics.

Coach

Nice, but you're not Wilma Rudolph, so hold on until it's pulled from you.

Bud

I'll check about the glove. We should let them get back to the lockers.

Coach

One minute. Remember we are outsiders, no college money, just strong minds---independents with a good record which means we are here to be shot down. Let's keep it going. Bud, remind them again where we stand in the elimination rounds.

Bud

Yesterday we smoked the 4 by 200 semis in relay. Tonight is our final. No one can come near the dust you leave behind. Porsche and Speed are in semifinals. Don't kill each other doing it. Either way, we have a first and second place win.

Coach

Porsche, I need to talk to you. Team, I'll see you in the locker.

Porsche

Can it wait until we get inside?

Coach

No.

Bud

(*Purposefully interrupts*) Coach, when should I tape Holly's knee, now or near race time?

Coach

When you find the time. Porsche, lets walk a bit. We need to talk about a few things.

PORSCHE follows away from the group, walking slowing, stopping on occasion, halts five feet away from COACH upstage and turns from facing him directly. They stand in darkness.

Holly

(*Disappointed*) OoooH. I wish the Coach didn't holler and get jumpy before a big race. He needs to check himself sometimes. Stuff about small things make my legs tense.

Jazmine

If he made love to you, you still wouldn't gain speed.

Holly

Jaz, can you stop the cut sometimes.

Rashida

(*Rises from the bleachers annoyed*) Why is she so important, that they to have private talks, as if they have a pact.

Bud

(*Gathering the towels, etc.*) It's his style of showing appreciation. She does carry the team a lot.

Jazmine

Never see me complain for attention.

Bud

There's complaint in every stride you take next to her.

Jazmine

I want to win my race again! After Coach recruited her, it's NOTHING but her, her, and her.

Bud

(*Calmly*) Easy, dig into yourself (*Touches her arm lightly*) You'll be surprised, you still got it.

Jazmine

(*Quickly steps aside*) Hands off. Bud, I'm in training.

Holly

You're always in training.

Jazmine

That's right and plan to stay that way. (*Breaks away and jogs off track downstage right*)

Bud

Got any steam to let off, Hot Rod?

Rashida

Not funny. (*Walks away moodily down the track and then off*)

Bud

(*Notices HOLLY still sitting on the bench, looking over shoulder at the COACH and PORSCHE for the COACH*) Holly, I'm not going in right now, maybe you should catch up with the others.

Holly

I'm waiting for the Coach. Anyway, what's wrong with my knee?

Bud

Nothing. Coach wants you to balance those

pretty legs. We tape one knee to make you think to use the other more. See you inside, okay.

Holly

(*Approaches seductively*) Putting me off so quickly?

Bud

Yes. You need to concentrate on lane turns. You may get faster times. (*Turns to pick up towels*)

Holly

You have a nice smile, Bud. It was the first thing I noticed when you joined the team.

Bud

Thanks, but I like my job more.

Holly

Aren't I part of the job? I'm not hard work.

Bud

You're right. Wrapping your knee is easy. See you inside.

Lights fade on BUD as he exits. HOLLY follows slowly. The lockers go dark.

Scene 5

Lights rise on COACH and PORSCHE on the track.

Porsche

What is it?

Coach

Lately, we haven't entered our meets on the same foot. I want to be sure we understand the importance of tonight.

Porsche

(*Angrily spins around to him*) I know what's important! I run and you don't.

Coach

I see!

Porsche

I feel it! ---I run hard. I run as hard as I can! Yet, I'm still a loser when I talk to you. I don't want to talk now because you're hyped over winning tonight, which means every little thing is wrong with me.

Coach

It's not intentional. Open up, talk to me...tell me what I need to do to keep our friendship.

Porsche

It's time for me to be my own coach. I want my own clock.

Coach

WHY? My program has worked for you. You're a star runner. What's not working for us.

Porsche

The Texas team was whispering about you

coaching there next year. *(She turns from him to exit)*

Coach

(Annoyed, he laughs) Ah, C'mon. They were psyching you. They would love to have me as their Coach. Striders is my heart.

Bud

(Enters and looks at PORSCHE as she passes to exit) Coach, we should confirm our entries.

Coach

(Calls to her) Let's talk later, Porsche.

Bud

A rumor's running wild she's been recruited by Eugene State. Full scholarship.

Coach

That's tomorrow's news. We just need tonight.

Lights fade to black as the men exit.

54

Scene
6

Lights rise on the locker room like a slap of hands. The runners enter with sounds of stadium fanfare in background.

Holly

I need my glove. (*Picks up sketch book*) I should do some glove designs.

Rashida

(*Annoyed, she paces around. Stops abruptly*) Oops, you keep going on and on about gloves. Stop. Winning's not with what's on your hand.

Holly

Neither is what you put on your feet but sneakers do count, don't they? I'm tired of the team bad mouthing my glove.

Jazmine

(*Starts a set of warm up exercises*) Superstition.

Holly

It is all luck. (*Pauses. Picks up her drawings*) I think the Coach will really like my track jackets. They're really sexy. The colors, oh, we'll really jump out front when we run. The entire stadium will see us…like…like bright stars.

PORSCHE enters and slumps on bench. She covers her face.

Holly

Breeze, look, my designs. Great, right. They're the Strider's new suits.

Porsche

Not going to be on the Strider's next year.

Rashida

What did the Coach want?

Porsche

Nothing. I need to see Bud. My ankle is swollen.

Holly

What! No, no, no.

Jazmine

Say it again. Say it AGAIN. SAY IT AGAIN.

Porsche

I am out. I can't put pressure on my foot.

Rashida

(*Kneels next to her*) Not enough to stop you from running the relay.

Jazmine

Yes, hurray Oakland, definitely on my side!

Holly

Affects you too.

Jazmine

It's fantastic!

Rashida

Is it serious? Will it put you out? How did it happen?

Porsche

Not sure. Maybe earlier. I. went out to see the sunrise. The lake was so magical. I wanted to walk, to loosen up, breathe. I tossed all night, not knowing how to work out the race in my mind. Then the sun began to peek over the hills. I don't know, the light and the sky, I began to run hard.

Jazmine

My sleep was sweet.

Porsche

Bet it was. You never cared about three other runners, how fast they will run, or pass, knowing no matter what they did, the end of the race depended on my winning it.

Jazmine

Or lose it.

Rashida

Went to jog?! Can't believe you.

Porsche

Same chances if I ran and fell in a race. Or pulled a muscle. It happens.

Holly

Why didn't you come back to the hotel? Why didn't you see the doctor?

Porsche

Why, why, why, why. Is there an answer. Can it change anything now? I was too ashamed to come back. I started not to come at all. There was no rush to face the team.

Jazmine

Find the Coach.

Holly

If she's not running. I'm not running. We can't win without her! (*Jumps straight off the bench*) That's it, we lost! It's all over.

Rashida

Holly, find the Coach. (*She pulls out her prayer cloth from the locker*) Go!

HOLLY *exits.*

Jazmine

Oh, not again, Hot Rod. Your psyche's blown and that noise sure won't bring it back.

Rashida

(*She ignores JAZMINE and holds her prayer cloth to her chest*) I need space, Speed. My mind is rocking. (*Paces*)

Jazmine

Clumsy let you down, didn't she? I got your back Ra.

Porsche

Who can trust you, Speed!?

Jazmine

Everyone, cause I am the only hope.

Rashida

(*Angry*) If you want me to say I need you, I need you, Jazmine. I want my medal tonight. I want to win so bad, I'll say I need you more than I ever needed her to win.

Porsche

You'd kiss the devil wouldn't you.

Rashida

Anything to be complete. This is my last race. My last season as a competitive runner. I'll never make the Olympics like you. I want to end strong.

Porsche

How have I stopped you? How has my pain stopped your dreams?

Rashida

We had plans. We were---

Porsche

We were nothing. I'm leaving Striders.

Rashida

Whether we win or lose is always on you! I gave you so many things, money, clothes.

Porsche

Ah, so your friendship was a loan, a debt. That winning was my way to pay to stay friends.

Rashida

What does that mean?! Can't twist the fact you are dumping us to quit.

Coach

(*Enters quietly, surprising the runners*)
Sounds like we're ready to meet the heat.

LIGHTS OUT

ACT II

Scene

7

Lights rise on the locker room.

Coach

(*Pretends*) Are we ready to meet the meet
(*No one responds*) Where's my team?

Rashida

Did you see, Holly? (*Sips water from a bottle*)

Coach

What are you drinking?

Rashida

(*Shakes bottle*) Doesn't matter. You need to deal with Breeze.

Coach

Please, no drug violations.

Rashida

It's only water.

COACH takes water bottle from RASHIDA to examine.

Jazmine

(*Begins stretches*) One...two...three... four....

Coach

Porsche, let's go, sneakers on. We have less than a half hour to line up at the gates.

Jazmine

That's the problem.

Coach

We <u>have no</u> problems tonight.

Jazmine

Tell him the good news, Breeze. Five...six... seven, eat my legs...

Rashida

(*Rapidly*) C, Bud can look at her ankle. I, I mean the team doesn't have time to worry over it.

Coach

Quiet please! What are we talking about?

Jazmine

(*Points to PORSCHE'S foot*). Own it.

Coach

What's wrong? Are you hurt?

Porsche

YES. YES. I'm human.

COACH steps back, stunned.

Jazmine

(*Moves to a far side and jogs quietly in place.*) Criss-cross, bring it to the ground.

Porsche

I twisted my foot on a rock this morning.

Coach

Can I see? *(She holds out leg for him to touch the ankle.*

COACH *kneels to look at ankle.*

Rashida

(Disturbed by this attention toward PORSCHE, she paces around the bench, stops, taps foot for emphasis) This is a definite waste of time. All this could have been avoided if you had taken my advice. I warned you she was running before meets last month.

Porsche

No one controls my work outs. If I feel the need to run to feel fit, it's not your worry.

Coach

(Stands, annoyed by JAZMINE's exercising) Stop moving, Speed!

Jazmine

This is part of my warm-up. Just get a
wheelchair and take her out.

Coach

Jazmine, I accept whatever you do is
serious, but not now! Everyone out.

*RASHIDA moves silently to the back of
locker area out of view.*

Jazmine

Only problem is, you can't see the
problem. (*Slams her locker shut and leaves*)

Porsche

Can't run.

Rashida

Yes, you can. (*Stands in front of COACH*)
If she doesn't run then all we did to get
here is blown away.

Coach

Rashida, this is not our finish line.

Rashida

She's trying to ruin you. She's leaving the school. It's an excuse to put the Striders down.

Porsche

It's my life, isn't? No one made me fast.

Coach

Stop!

Rashida

It's all over the stadium, Breeze is leaving Striders.

COACH rises and steps back and looks at PORSCHE in disbelief.

Rashida

When are you going to tell him? (*Pacing*)

Coach

Are you jumping the gun on us?

Rashida

Yeah, she is!

Porsche

I can speak for myself.

Coach

Rashida, please leave.

Rashida

Should I leave the team too?

Coach

Please Ra, give us ten.

She stares angrily at PORSCHE then COACH, then exits.

Coach

(*Apologetic, after a pause*) Ah, let's start again like most civil people. Good evening.

Porsche

Same.

Coach

Anything to tell me?

Porsche

No.

Coach

How are your counseling sessions with Mrs. Carson?

Porsche

Great.

Coach

When did you see her last?

Porsche

As soon as we got back to Oakland.

Coach

That's a lie.

Porsche

Maybe it is. What's your point?

Coach

She hasn't seen you in a month. I had a hunch you stopped talking to her when you started showing up late for workouts, withdrawn, agitated.

Porsche

She's your idea not mine. I don't need her to work out my sanity. Being independent doesn't mean I am failing myself.

Coach

Then why are you hurt. Or is the injury a fake, an excuse to feel sorry for yourself.

Porsche

Not an excuse. Chance of falling, or pulling a muscle is always there. When it happens. It happens. I have limits.

Coach

You're too competitive to sit out tonight. It will eat you inside forever.

Porsche

I'll run when I am ready.

Coach

Sure, but your body has a clock, and a solid chance for gold. Back to Mrs. Carson.

Porsche

Not going back. She talks sideways about my mother, my father, why I dropped out of school, how the club has brought me scholarships. Tired of it. I don't feel her, and she doesn't feel me.

Coach

There's a roar in the stands waiting to holler your name. Can you feel that? You have a winning streak. One more time.

Porsche

Who'll guarantee I will be able to run afterwards.

Coach

Afterwards you'll be the fastest runner around. This is our shot. It may never come again. *(Rises)*

Porsche

Not a flat tire you can patch to roll on to another medal. (*Angrily*) I am leaving the club.

Coach

(*On his feet, he strolls a bit, after a few beats, tense)* You can quit. But not until you try to overcome your pain. It's hard. But you have to do it. Once I was the best around, but I didn't have a record. The closest I came was five yards from the finish. A man rode my heels down the stretch. Kicking, splattering stinging cinder grit about my legs. A runner on my right nearly rubbed my shoulder raw, but I was winning. It was mine. (*Whispering*) Get the record--break the record kept pounding as hard as my heart. The crowd roared. IT WAS NOW. All my muscles strained as I lunged forward to take more lead. My lungs blazed. (*Let's out a tight breath*) Then poww---a shot went off in my leg. I fell–through my tears, everyone rushed pass. After, too afraid to push again even to become what I once was. If you nurse the pain tonight, it will finish you. Refuse to let it defeat you.

Porsche

Why fall in front of that stadium wanting to be inside me, thrilled by a speeding body. Why run, why disappoint them. I can't win.

Why destroy myself for a trophy or a medal?
> **Coach**

Fantasy. They are real...bona-fide symbols of who you are. (*Turns from her*)
> **Porsche**

You can't make me run.
> **Coach**

(*Turns back to her quickly*) No, but if you want to stay on my team as a sound and sane runner, then you will.
> **Porsche**

I quit.
> **Coach**

Not until I cut you. Now stand up.
> **Porsche**

What for?
> **Coach**

For yourself on your feet. Quick. Break the wall.

Porsche

NO.

Coach

STAND! On your feet.

Porsche

(*Shifts indolently on the bench.*) If I stand, I will walk out.

Coach

WALK THEN. Just get off that bench!
(*She rises slowly, stunned by COACH*) Walk!

Porsche

(*She takes a small step to exit*) I'm not running.

Coach

Faster...more... come on...this will work out the tightness...(*He stands in front of the exit. She limps around from him*) Feels fine...lift the knees more. That's it. Keep going.

Porsche

(*Turns to him*) Get a grip. You are not my father or my man.

Coach

I am everything, who fostered you to this day.

Porsche

I'm sick of you and this team! (*She kicks over the bench*)

Coach

If you leave. I will (*Steps in front of her*)

Porsche

----do nothing. You can't change my record. You didn't make me fast.

HOLLY and BUD rush into the locker room interrupting the COACH from touching PORSCHE. BUD has a towel around his neck and carries a gear bag and a roll up mat.

Holly

Coach, we've looked all over for you.

Coach

Bud, (*Picking up the bench, straightens self into a more professional posture*) See what you can do. (*Exits*)

Bud

(*Drops a gear bag on bench*) What has my bunny done to herself? (*Rolls out mat and helps her lower onto it*)

Holly

Bunny?

Bud

Easy, on your side...slow (*She turns onto side to face audience*)

Holly

(*Sitting on the bench*) If she was a horse you would have to shoot her, wouldn't you?

Bud

Knew this would happen. (*Squeezing ankle*) Where's the pain? Here?

Porsche

AAwwhhh!

Holly

He hardly touched you.

Bud

Holly, you need to start warming up with the team.

Holly

I'm already warmed-up. Besides you have to tape my knee, remember. She's not the only one who needs attention. (*Takes off jacket, revealing a sports bra.*) It's hot in here.

Porsche

(*Shakes her head*) Oops, no need to honey up Bud.

Bud

And Bud, has priorities, meaning you have to go. (*Rises to escort her out*)

Holly

I'm your witness. Porsche has lots of fantasies. Troubling ones, you know. Like her ankle.

Bud

I'll take my chances. Let's go.

Holly

Why can't I be here? I'm not in the way. I want to watch. You want me too, don't you Porsche. (*Sits on bench*)

Porsche

She leaves or I will.

Holly

My knee, remember Bud.

Bud

I'll check your knee as soon as I am finished. (*He gently escorts her to the side exit*)

Holly

Promise?

Porsche

Guaranteed.

Holly

I'll be waiting. (*She smiles loving as she waves bye, exits*)

Porsche

(*Turning onto her back*) How bad is it? What can be done?

Bud

(*Kneels next to her*) A whole lot last night.

Porsche

I want to run...then I don't... my mind is jumping lanes. I'm losing it straight out of top of my head.

Bud

(*Massages her legs*) The nicest body I ever wanted to touch.

Porsche

Are you listening?

Bud

Every breath. calm down, inhale gently, go ahead. (*Exaggeratedly*) Right...relax. How do my hands feel?

Porsche

Okay.

Music rises softly in background as the lights dim.

Bud

From the pleasure I'm getting, it has to be great. (*His hands begin to move inch by inch up her legs*) Relax...this body's as fine as a needle point.

Porsche

Feels more like a broken tip.

Bud

Lean and defined...no fat to take the shock of overwork. (*She tosses a bit*) (*She lies with her eyes closed, releasing tension as BUD continues to massage her*) Once I touch *you*, my hands move without my will. I'd massaged you through the long night, if you would have only come to me...sapping tiredness and tension from your slim body, charging every muscle to your heart with (*seductively*) the positive flow from my fingertips.

Porsche

STOP.

Bud

Don't want to.

Porsche

(Sits up, grabs his hands) Stop. Take your hands off me.

Bud

(Stops) You want it. But you can't say yes, can you?

Porsche

I can, when I want to. I said no-- No, once and only once.

Bud

(Sits back away from her) Always your way.

Porsche

Yes, only my way. Since you came on board, you keep trying to make me. I'm not Holly. I need more than sweet words and soft hands.

Bud

Well then, let's put some ice on the culprit. *(He slaps the ice bag* on *her ankle)*

Porsche

Ouch!

Bud

Not too much swelling. Bet you went tipping straight off the ground flying to Mars or was it, Venus?

Porsche

The way you're slapping my foot around, does it matter.

Bud

Try me.

Porsche

I broke a record this morning. I felt this tremendous surge of energy. I know I beat my best time.

Bud

Doesn't mean a thing unless you're timed in a meet. Could've been tonight.

You're a lot of runner, but to best your record means you ran fast as a man. And that is a long way before a woman does.

Porsche

Okay, sexist. Then I'm an exception. (*Attempts to shift away*)

Bud

(*Pulls her leg back*) Not as much as you think. Stay still.

Porsche

I'm a winner because I push limits, not by lying back and being ruled.

Bud

(*Taping ankle*)I watch how you win. Riding and kicking. A challenge to conquer something or someone otherwise there's no gain, no respect when it's easy. Here, have it, makes you weak to receive.

Porsche

Receive what? Respect doesn't get passed around easy, learned afer my father died my family became dirt, gossip.

Bud

I heard the business was a cover.

Porsche

He was decent. He earned his money selling insurance. Neighbors made up lies he was shot at his desk because he sold drugs, was in prostitution, laundered money. Lies. No one wanted us around. No one invited me to their home or wanted me around.

Bud

Rashida did.

Porsche

Sometimes. But I could never say no. Could not get angry with her. Scared she dump me. I need no one when I run. At the finish line, it's all about me.

Bud

(*He grabs her foot to tickle it*) And tonight. Say you'll run! Say it.

Porsche

(*She twists, tries to pull away*) Leave me alone.

Bud

The track star or the woman?

Porsche

My foot! Stop tickling!

Bud

(Rises to gather things) Okay, Ms. Extraordinary, see you on the track.

Porsche

(Rises to sit on the bench) Wish I was ordinary. No one expecting anything extra from a simple me.

Bud

Okay, Ms. Simple, do what is yours. Like everyone else, running their distance to win personal goals in the time they have. (*Collects gear bag and mat*) Anything to say to C? (*She shakes head no. He exits.*)

LIGHTS OUT

Scene

8

Crowd sounds are heard as lights rise on the three runners who enter and stand on the track.

Jazmine

Hey, let's do a quickie, keep our heat up. How about it, Ra?

Holly

Nooo. Nothing but a work horse, Speed.

Jazmine

Not a big deal, Oops. All the other teams are doing light sprints.

Holly

So, what. We already had a warmup. What if

one of my legs----

Jazmine

----you'll *never ever* pull a muscle!

Rashida

(*Uptight, paces the track*) Stop shouting. Let's talk how to run our relay without Porsche.

Holly

She has to run.

Jazmine

No, she doesn't. We need a new strategy without her.

Holly

We need a baton.

Jazmine

Forget the baton. Forget Breeze. She's saving it for her new team.

Holly

Hater. She's not leaving. How do you know? Whispers in the wind.

Jazmine

Everyone is talking about it. Let's work

out the relay now. What do you say, Ra?

Holly

I didn't hear her say she wasn't.

Jazmine

Has she ever told you the truth. She is done with the Striders.

Rashida

She is not. Just shut up.

Jazmine

Get yourself right! I am not Oops!

Rashida

Then stop the up in your face psych out!

Holly

That's it. We've lost.

Jazmine

If we lose, it's his fault because he believes Breeze is the only one who can win. And has you so doped you can't without her. I don't need her.

The COACH enters the track on the opposite of the stage unaware of the team, frequently checks his wristwatch.

Rashida

There's the Coach. Let's talk to him.

Jazmine

Not wasting my time. I'm in a single event which I intend to win, by myself. (*Exits*)

Rashida

Coming, Oops? Please...

Holly

Nah...Protesting to Coach is a waste. The deal is to talk to Breeze. Wait up, Speed! (*Trots off after JAZMINE*)

Scene 9

Lights rise on COACH as RASHIDA approaches softly.

Rashida

Coach...I...the team and I decided we need to have a honest discussion with you.

Coach

(*Distant*) What is it, Ra?

Rashida

We think you've let the situation run away from your control. You're our Coach, the team's coach, not just Porsche's.

Coach

My control has limits.

Rashida

What's next without her? We're in this to win, too.

Coach

I'll handle it in time. (*Side steps Rashida*)

Rashida

We don't have time. It's your fault. (*Turns toward him as he passes her*) You gave in more to her than me— or the team.

Coach

I gave everyone what they needed.

Rashida

What about wanted.

Coach

It's not about what you wanted.

Rashida

Why not. It was always her. She got more attention in workouts...praise, and—

Coach

And demands and pain! Did you want that too! (*Turns to her quickly*)

Rashida

YES.

Coach

I thought you were satisfied with the way I handled your training.

Rashida

What about me. My feelings. I train as hard. Where is my specialness—

Coach

You're kind and helpful. You're my team, but she's my runner. You can't race the way she does. If you could, you would understand our relationship.

Rashida

Means nothing.

Coach

Can you try harder if I yell? Can you convert

pressure into a better performance? Or will you cry, will you pout. That is the difference. My challenge to do more, do better, makes her (*Pauses thoughtfully*) makes air under her feet.

Rashida

When your great runner falls, will you see your real team.

Coach

Let's pass on this, Ra.

> *BUD enters the track and trots toward the COACH and RASHIDA, breaking the tension.*

Bud

Can I have a second with you, Coach.

> *The COACH steps away from RASHIDA, who stands disappointed then exits.*

Scene 10

Coach

Is she steady on her feet?

Bud

Looks like a sprain. I wrapped it tight.

Coach

Can she last the whole race?

Bud

Iced it but it is a gamble.

Coach

Do we have a pain killer under the radar that will work fast enough without disqualifying her race?

Bud

Better she knows her limit than run and fall.

Coach

We have to place.

Bud

Come on, Coach. You have other runners.

Coach

It's her no, makes me unsure of my coaching, my training.

Bud

Come on. Her no sounds awfully quiet next to the years it took to get in this meet.

Coach

I wanted us to move on together.

Bud

Is that your worry. When are you are going to tell the team?

Coach

(*Angry*)Tell them what! No win tonight means, tomorrow I'll be cut down with rumors of money, drugs, male domination of female athletes. How I used poor disadvantaged way wards to make a name.

Bud
They deserve to know.
Coach
Not tonight. Not tonight.
Bud
Let me set the doctor up. I'll meet you inside.

He exits as lights slowly fade on COACH.

Scene
11

Lights rise on PORSCHE in the locker room walking around slowly, testing the pain. JAZMINE and HOLLY charge in.

Holly
If you can walk, you can run, Breeze.
Jazmine
Think she's sulking over losing the 200 to me.
(*Slides on bench to annoy*)

Porsche

You can have it. I am off the team. (*Moves down bench away from JAZMINE who follows her movement on bench*)

Holly

You can't quit like that.

Porsche

I just did. Leave me alone, Speed. Leave the lockers.

Jazmine

Don't move Oops. (*Rises*) The lockers are equal territory. There's no stars in here.

Holly

(*Clears throat to change to a pleading tone*) If you're not running, can I use your glove?

Porsche

I didn't bring my glove. Let go of the crutch. It's a bust to need something more than yourself. Stop needing me for what you want.

Holly

(*Flops dejectedly on the bench*) If you

don't run, we won't win. Then the Striders will be a could've been.

Porsche
Try to be the could have been without me.

Holly
Ooooohh, who wants to hear what I should be.

RASHIDA enters quietly.

Jazmine
What's up, Hot Rod. You look beat.

Rashida
Bud told me the Coach signed on to State.

Holly
So, are we going too. He's going to take us, isn't he?

Jazmine

We're on our own, Oops.

Rashida

Part of the deal is that you are GOING WITH HIM.

Holly

Is that it? Sitting on us to burn him?

Porsche

No. I am not in his dealings.

Jazmine

Now it clicks. Nikki at the Express was writing me up when he rushed and pulled me away. She asked if were getting scholarships—

Holly

(*Flops dejected*) OOGGHHH, what's the use of anything? I wished so hard for this day and it's all bad. (*Picks up drawings and rips*) He lied about my designs.

Jazmine

STOP, OOPS. They are good. Take them to someone else.

Coach

(*Enters, having heard the last lines, attempts cheer, but it is strained*) Glad to see everyone's spirit is up. It's all love. All love (*Everyone stands wooden*)

Jazmine

Excuse me, Coach, feel a nervous stomach. Need to make a pit stop. (*Slides pass him to exit*)

Coach

Make it quick.

Holly

I need a pair of gloves, Coach.

Coach

Bud's taking care of it.

Rashida

Did you hear, Breeze is leaving the team?

PORSCHE *rises to exit.*

Coach
(*Ignoring PORSCHE as long as possible*) Okay runners, we have little time left before the race.

Rashida
Did you hear me?

Coach
Doesn't matter, we are the winners, aren't we? (*Does not look at her directly*) Okay, listen up, we have not lost this relay in a year, and we will not tonight.

Holly
We will if we get the inside lane, and Breeze quits. I know I will fly off the ramp on a turn.

Coach
Nonsense, (*Responds directly to HOLLY ignoring RASHIDA and PORSCHE*) Negotiate them as I told you.

Holly

What about my designs for new suits?

Coach

I will not let you down, Holly. We have to focus on the relay.

Rashida

You're lying to us.

Holly

What about Breeze?

Coach

(*Never looking at her*) She's good for one race. The relay if she has a change of heart.

Porsche

I quit.

Holly

AAAAHHHHH Porsche. Why? It's our last race.

Rashida

LET HER GO.

Coach

We have a race to run! Keep your minds on
it.

Porsche

I race to win, not run to lose.

Coach

Then it's settled. Lucinda's warming up
down the hall, there's too much confusion in
here.

Holly

Lucinda can't race! She can't even walk. We
will lose.

Coach

Whether we win or lose, we're going to
show our faces.

Holly

C'mon, Breeze. I've seen you win on a
broken toe. Please try for our last race
together.

Porsche

Even if I did, the team would lose

momentum worrying whether I would fall or quit.

Loudspeaker

(Is heard from offstage) Good evening, ladies, gentlemen, and athletes. Welcome to the 27th International Invitational games in Oakland, California.

Fanfare is heard in and out of the remaining dialogue. Everyone takes a few beats to consider the moment has arrived.

Coach

Well, I'll be on the east side of the track. *(He moves to exit)*

Porsche

Quitting is easy, isn't it Coach.

Coach

(Returning) Maybe and maybe not.

Porsche

Maybe?

Holly

(*Happy*) She means yes. Don't you?

Porsche

I didn't say yes.

Holly

(*Excited*) It's yes again. Did you hear her, Rashida? We'll smash tonight. Then our invites to race in Europe is on.

Coach

Ra is first, Oops is second, you're third, and Speed is last.

Rashida

Wait, Porsche runs the last leg. You can't screw us around.

Coach

The positions are the same. The distances are all the same.

Porsche

The fourth is a takers. I might drop the baton

if I had to give it to her.

Coach

You're too risky to run the final lap.

Porsche

I know more than Speed how to push and take the tape.

Holly

Oh, Coach ---It's a jinx to change us now.

Coach

We can win with you, Porsche, or lose without you. It doesn't matter. We are going to run tonight.

Loudspeaker

with teams across the states.

Rashida

Let her, Coach I don't think I can run a different leg. The strategies different.

Coach

I think Jazmine deserves a chance to run anchor. She has a strong finish.

Porsche

Then I'm not running.

Coach

Good, makes things easier.

Holly

Coach, please.

Rashida

She's willing to run.

Coach

Because we don't NEED HER.

Rashida

Do you need us? Really, do you really need us anymore?

Holly

You just said it's not whether we win or lose.

Coach

We will not lose. We are winning.

Loudspeakers

with first class teams. Tonight are finals in the 100, 200, indoor.

Porsche

It's your medal!

Coach

(*Infuriated*) Yes, I want it but I will not kneel and kiss your----(*Holds back words*)!

Rashida

Oh no. Coach, you're wrong. The whole team agrees--

Coach

This is not the whole team, and if it was, what I say goes. I've coached 15 years to get this kind of recognition. 15 years to put a winning team together. Not easy when the best went to scholarship schools. So I took money off my table to satisfy each and everyone of your whims. SO WHAT I say goes--- Not what you think or want–

Rashida

Well, scratch my name. The vibes aren't right for running. (*She sits on the bench next to PORSCHE*)

Coach
And you, Holly?
Holly
Guess so.
Coach
Well, hell, forfeit!

COACH turns in silence to exit.

Loudspeaker
Before we begin these exciting races. A few
announcements from the athletic ---
Bud
(*Enters meeting COACH*) Ah, I set the doc up.
Is she ready?
Holly
BudDD.
Coach
(*Very abrupt and* off) Ask her.
Holly
(*Rushing*) BUD we can't race!

Bud
Why? What happened?
Porsche
You can run, Oops.
Holly
Don't push me. (*Stamps her foot*)
Rashida
It's more like we don't want to.
Bud
We who?
Holly
I do.
Rashida
The team, Bud!
Bud
What about you the RUNNER?
Rashida
I'm a part of a team.
Bud
Do you the runner, want to? (*No response*)
DO YOU?!

Rashida

Yes! But he has to concede to us sometimes and stop demanding his way.

Bud

Coach's only demand was that each of you be proud of your bodies and worthy of attention. *(Flustered)* I bet you'll never find the respect he has brought you to tonight...in two more lifetimes.

Porsche

We gave him as much back. He used me, the team.

Bud

Oh well, So, we all lose? (*He slaps the floor with towel for emphasis*)

Holly

I don't want to lose, Bud. It's all a loss. He lied about my suit designs. (*Tears up the newspaper*) The paper was right.

Jazmine

(*Enters*) Why the heavy squat? Talk

somebody! Hot Rod, where's Coach?

Holly

I love the Coach! He lied. He's leaving and and he promised me.

Bud

No, Holly.

Jazmine

Porsche vamped y'all or something? ---------

Bud

Stop giving the love for yourselves to him. Stop sitting scared to face you can do it. It can happen. Only needing to say I want to, I can, I will----

Loudspeaker

Will everyone rise for the anthem '

Jazmine

The games are on! I'm out of here before I catch something

Holly

(*Tears up more newspaper*) You can't run!

Jazmine

Are you crazy? Stop tearing up that paper.

Rashida

If we run, he wins.

Bud

If you run, you win. You're not going to stop that man's shot at college coaching.

Rashida

And us? Where do we go? We have rights. –

Jazmine

Rights about what? What has that to do with racing?

Bud

Stay with it, Speed. The race is on in a few. (*Starts to leaves*)

Holly

Don't go, Bud. Get Coach.

Bud

He is not coming back. Whatever he said should not stop you from going out there and getting what you earned. (*Exits*)

Jazmine

Spit it out. What's the boycott about?

Holly

First the Coach wanted to use Lucinda. Then Porsche said she'd run but he wanted to switch us up in the relay. Porsche said no, Rashida said no...and I guess I'm with them.

Rashida

Don't guess. Be there.

Porsche

You can run.

Rashida

Legs up.

Jazmine

Count me out of the seance, preance. I have a single heat and I intend to win it.

Dead silence falls on the lockers. HOLLY is very jumpy. COACH enters the track and freezes on the sidelines in a spotlight.

Porsche

Whatever.

Jazmine

Whatever — I'm not giving this one up for no principle or person. (*Runs off*)

Holly

SPEED, DON'T LEAVE. Give me a hand to hand first. (*Stands to break away from the two on the bench*)

Jazmine

(*Turns back and gives Holly a pound on her fist*) Yo, Oops, pound it in the ground. Get out of here. (*Exits*)

Loudspeaker

(*Noise of fanfare crackles behind announcement*) There are several outstanding races tonight. The Striders are expected to continue their winning streak for 35th time tonight-------

Holly

(*Swings arms, not knowing what to do, anxious begins stepping backward toward exit, timid, drums rumble*) Okay team. They will know we are not running in a minute. So what are we going to do?

Porsche

Run, Oops. Run.

Holly

Are you trying to push me?

Porsche/Rashida

YES!

Loudspeaker

They have not officially lined up at the starting gates. They are the favors—

Holly

(*Moving closer to exit*) That's us. They are calling us. Sorry Breeze, -- but...but...I would do the same, especially after Coach duped us. It's just one more race, one more win. (*Feels guilty and embarrassed*) You'll always be a winner to me.

Porsche

Just go.

BUD joins the COACH on the track.

Rashida
He's not worth the praise? It's our glory.

JAZMINE joins COACH and BUD.

Bud
(*She raises her foot for him to tap her sneaker with a baton*) A touch of luck.
Loudspeaker
There are changes in the field. There is no word if the Striders, the phenomenal team from California---

This announcement hits RASHIDA hard. She rises quickly, paces. A blast of cheering comes through the locker.

Rashida
Why is the crowd yelling so loud?

Loudspeaker

.... will be running------Correction, the team line up is not completed....

Rashida

Are they announcing us? *(Stops to listen)*

HOLLY trots onto the track.

Porsche

Legs up, Rashida. DON'T use me against the Coach. Have guts to run without me. Cut me free.

Bud

(Handing HOLLY a glove) Oops, a glove for you.

RASHIDA paces around the locker.

Holly

Keep it, Bud.

Jazmine

Your head and hand finally connected.

Holly

(*Quickly*) To win!

Loudspeaker

There's no official word as to whether the world record holder in the 200 meter will run. It appears only one of the Striders is in that race…

> *COACH looks at his watch then BUD wondering how much time they have. They freeze.*

*****

Inside the locker.

Rashida

What's the matter with you? Why are you

stepping in my way?

Porsche

(*Rises to step in her path*) Your body's talking, Ra. It wants to run. I knew for a long time you wished there will be a day when the team will not need me. Then Coach will see and appreciate your stuff. Do it now.

Coach

We can't wait any longer to confirm. (*Calling toward the exit*) Rashida!

Rashida

Yes! I hated the love they had in their eyes for you. Yes, I wanted the shine they gave you. Yes, I know I could not make this team, if I was not a friend. Wasting a lot of myself, hiding either the hate or the love from showing.

Porsche

Guess what? I hate you, too. (*PORSCHE pushes her*) Show him, it was never him or me that made you a runner. (*She pushes her again*)

Loudspeaker

The record holder, international world champion for three years straight in the 200 meters is injured----

Rashida

And you...

Loudspeaker

No word as to whether the team will run with an alternate. We await the official calls to check in. They're the announcing the Striders' now. They are racing -----------

Porsche

I have tomorrow.

Rashida

Legs up. (*Exits*)

PORSCHE paces the locker as the lights begin to fade.

Loudspeaker

It is official. The Striders will enter the relay with a new line -up. Texas Cats are in lane one. Striders lane two, lane three is Colorada----

Music rises. RASHIDA joins the team.

Jazmine

For a minute thought she buried you.

Holly

It's all good. Legs up!

Coach

Is she coming?

Rashida

Shrugs) Does it matter?

Coach

No.

Porsche

(*Rises to exit*)---scarred, too afraid to even push again... even to become what

I once was. No--what I was-wanting a to be loved, to be respected at a finish line. Today there is no love for me. I won, needing no one, no one to push me, to force me to hurt myself for their love. I have tomorrow, and the next day, and the next race. (*Limps quickly off to join team but does not race*)

Music rises as the lights fade

Loudspeaker

All quiet in the in-field. SssssHHHH! On your mark, set, GO. (*A starter gun is fired*)

FINALE RUN

Each runner passes the baton as they take a curtain call.

THE END

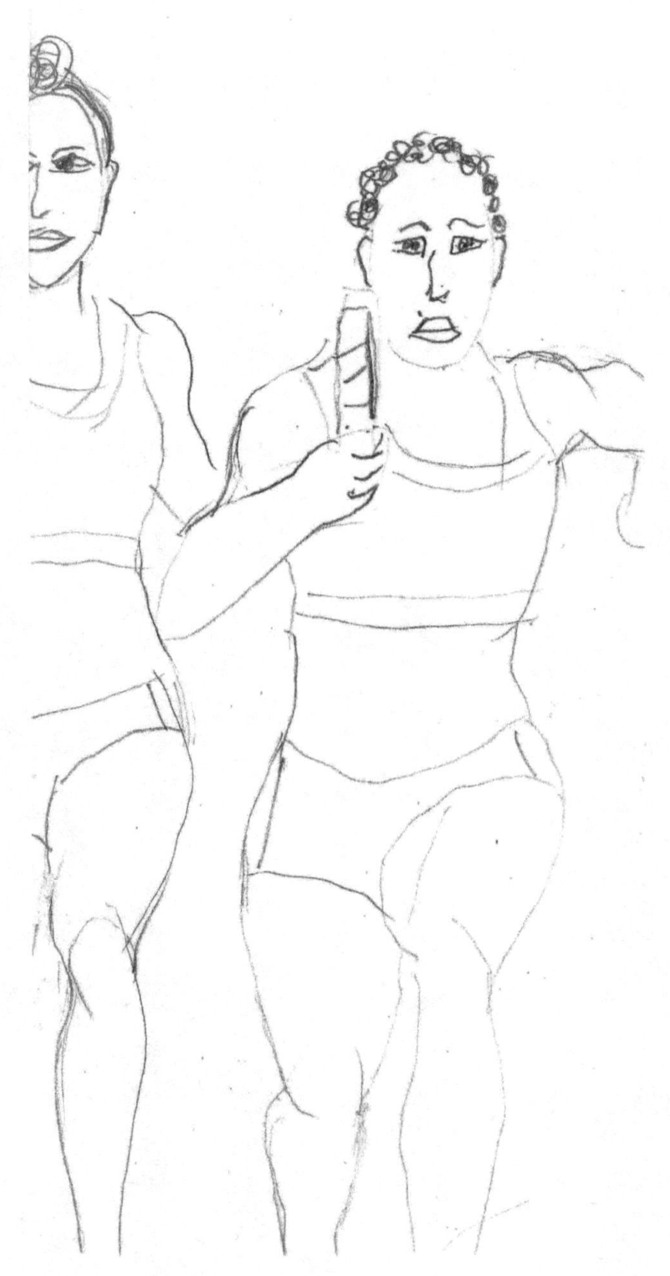

ACKNOWLEDGMENT

The Striders Team is a revision of the play *Run'ers* developed through the Frank Silvera Writers Workshop and LaMaMa ETC in New York City. It was produced in Oakland, California at the Malonga Arts Center, the Open Eye Theater and the New Federal Theater, New York City.

The play received two New York Theater Audelco Awards, for audience excellence; one for writing and another for supporting actress.

Much appreciation and enduring gratitude to all the actors, actresses, directors, creative designers for their work on the play.

Special thanks to all the great track athletes who shared their insight with me.

WRITER

The author was part of the booming black theater scene in New York City for several year. She wrote the play living in a third floor walk up in the East Village, on 9th and Second Avenue. Once a very creative place to live.

She has a M.A. in Theater from Hunter College and a B.A. Psychology from New York University.